THE JOURNEY OF CATTAIL

Written & Illustrated by

BARBARA A. PALMER

BP
FOLKART PRESS

www.bpfolkartpress.com

Treasure your journey

Barbara A. Palmer

*For my husband John, the frame maker, for my daughter Brooke
and for all the friends I've encountered on my life's journey.*

*Special thanks are due to Neil Montanus for his photographic
reproductions of my art, my assistant Debbie Breed who helped edit
the text and Jennifer Meagher for her guidance and enthusiasm.*

Library of Congress Catalog number:
2003095695

ISBN 0-9728228-0-1

Art: Theorem Painting on Velvet
This book was written, illustrated and produced by Barbara A. Palmer
Design and layout by Patricia Tyler Cornelius
based on a design by Barbara A. Palmer.
Display type set in Mambo and text type set in Timbrel.
Printed in China

*For those who seek
The white tippity tail,
Watch as Cattail ages
And follow his trail
Over velvety pages
While he makes friends
With fellow felines
And Fido.*

A portion of the proceeds from the sale of this book will be donated to The Humane Society.

One spring morning as the sun spilled golden and warm,

Cattail began his journey.

Cattail was a tiny black cat with a very long tail, tipped white on the end. He pranced over hills and tumbled down dales and chased his own shadow into a large red barn.

Inside the barn, three cats were stretched out on a carpet of sweet smelling hay. Their names were...

Annie, Danny and Fanny Cat...

and they found the young black cat's tail very amusing. Instead of chasing their own tails, they chased Cattail's.

Even Fido, the watch dog, would join the chase when he wasn't chasing something else.

The next day, Cattail scampered up to the large yellow farm house where he met...

Gary, Harry and Terry Cat.

Down the road Cattail found another farm with quilts for sale. Napping in a basket were...

Jill and Bill and Sue and Lew Cat.

They loved to play hide-and-go-seek among the quilts flapping in the breeze. While Cattail did his best to hide...

his tail would not.

The summer dance of dragon flies drew Cattail to

Squash Blossom Brooke.

A covered bridge beckoned Cattail as he wove through fenced sunflowers, across the quilted landscape to

Apple Sauce Creek.

11

A crisp, cool autumn moon called Cattail as he passed through

Crabby Cove.

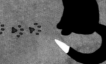

13

On

Stone House Hill,

Cattail tasted his first fluffy snowflake.

15

It was a cold, snowy wind that blew Cattail to a warm hearth in Quilters Cove.

He spent the winter with...

Matthew, Margaret, and Maggie Cat.

His long tail kept them all warm as the fire became embers late each night.

In spring, Cattail's journey took him to Tillie's Tea Room.
He and...

Justin, Dustin and Julie Cat...

were served crumpets, tea and johnnycakes on fine
china dishes.

$\mathcal{O}$n a curious, early summer day, Cattail followed...

Barry, Sherry and Carrie Cat...

into the red school house. They commenced to play among the desks, books and inkwells. Soon there were blue paw prints everywhere. When the school bell rang, they all bounded out the window.

Cattail sped down the road alone.

It was a sultry mid-summer day when Cattail paused at the crest of the hill. At the bottom of the hill was...

Karen Cat.

Karen Cat was all black with a white tip on her tail and when Cattail saw her...

he knew his journey was over.

Cattail and Karen had many kittens. All were named after friends Cattail had made on his journey.

Annie, Danny and Fannie Cat...

Gary, Harry and Terry Cat...

Jill, Bill, Sue and Lew Cat...

Matthew, Margaret, and Maggie Cat...

Justin, Dustin and Julie Cat...

Barry, Sherry and Carrie Cat...

And the smallest kitten they named

Fido.